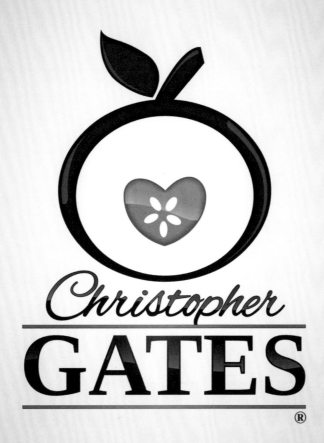

Published by

Auspicious
Ambitions

Unwind. Up, Up, and Away!
Text copyright © 2017 by Christopher Gates
Illustrations by Javier Ratti
Illustration copyright © 2018 Christopher Gates
Social and Emotional Learning (SEL) Competencies © 2017 CASEL
The Apple Heart's Core, Auspicious Ambitions and Foundation logos are
trademarks or registered trademarks of Christopher Gates

ISBN 978-0-9889739-5-4

First Edition

In dedication to the captivating, energetic, and enthusiastic children I will have someday, as well as the amazing, and precious children around the world.

May you grow up to be kind, confident, empathetic, and well-rounded lifelong learners!

unwind
Up, Up, and Away!

Christopher Gates
Author

Javier Ratti
Illustrator

Sometimes I feel like I'm surrounded by darkness.
I feel so lost, so out of control.

I am surrounded by emotions of
anger, sadness, frustration, and fear,
Ugly creatures closing in.

They pounce and clasp,
    Tying and squeezing all they can...

I am stuck with nowhere to go.
What's going on? How do I get out?

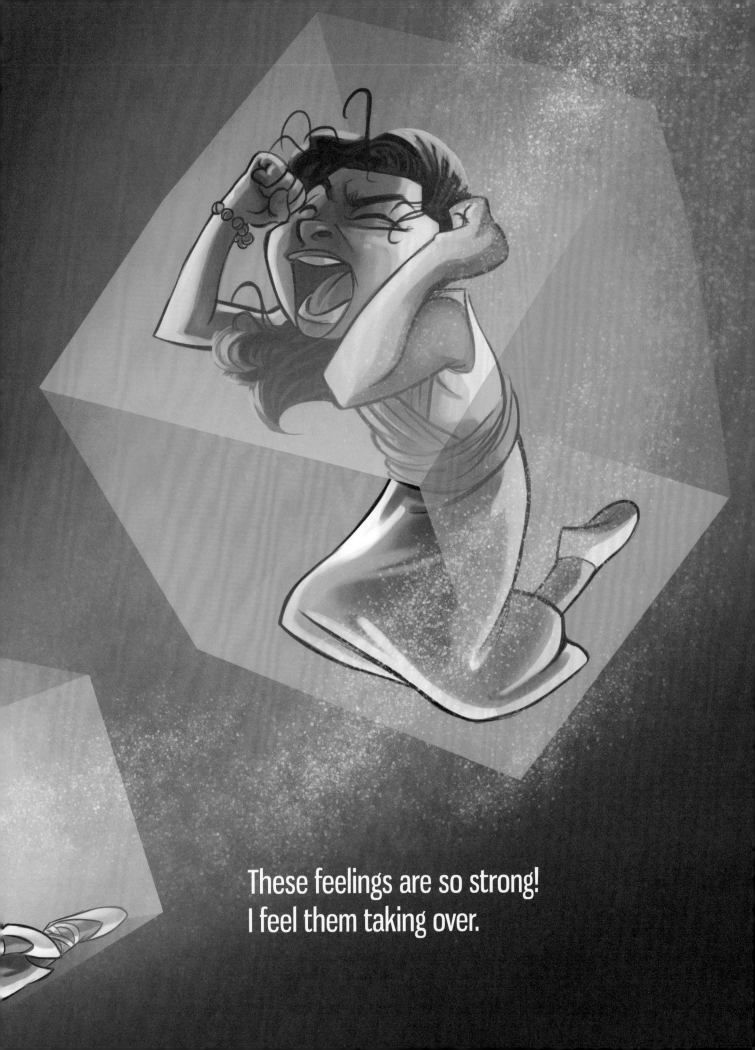

These feelings are so strong!
I feel them taking over.

In these moments, I must remember
that I have more power than I think.

Within me, I have the power - Yes
Superpowers to be set free.

With the power of mindfulness, I take a moment
to notice the emotions running through me.

I look straight at each monster
and recognize how I am feeling.

Before the monsters squeeze me tighter,
and steam gushes out of my ears,

I take another moment
and tell myself to unwind.

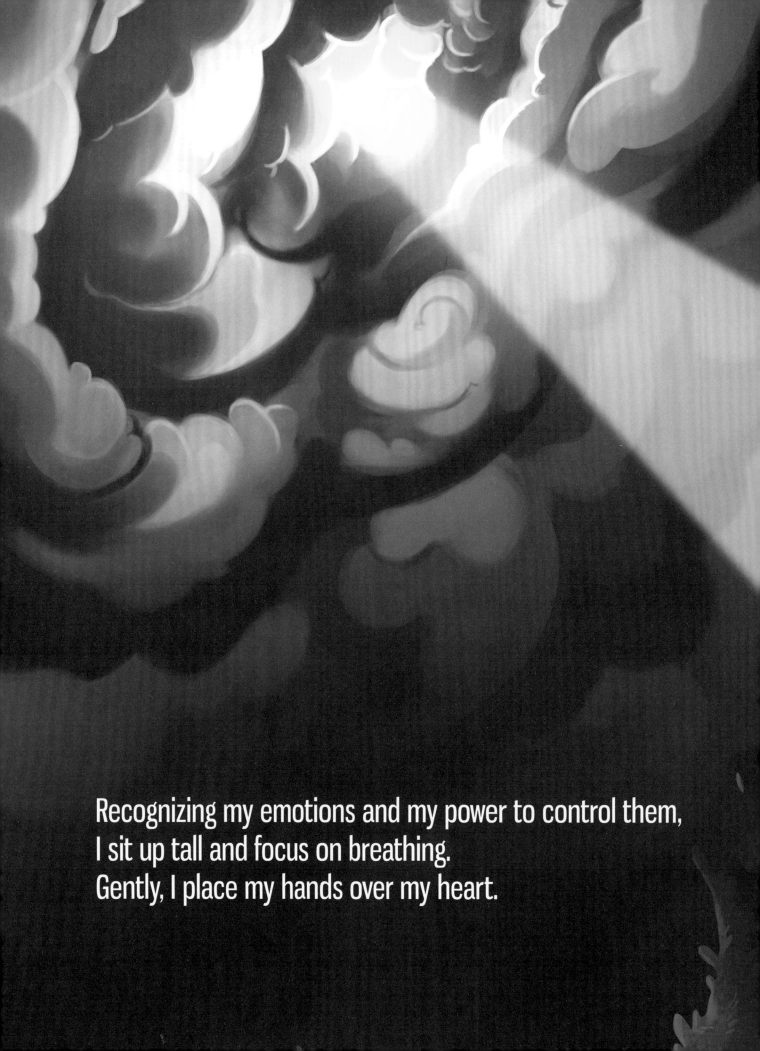

Recognizing my emotions and my power to control them,
I sit up tall and focus on breathing.
Gently, I place my hands over my heart.

I breathe in and breathe out.
Slowly, I clear my mind of all around me.

I stretch my arms out
Starting with my left, then my right.

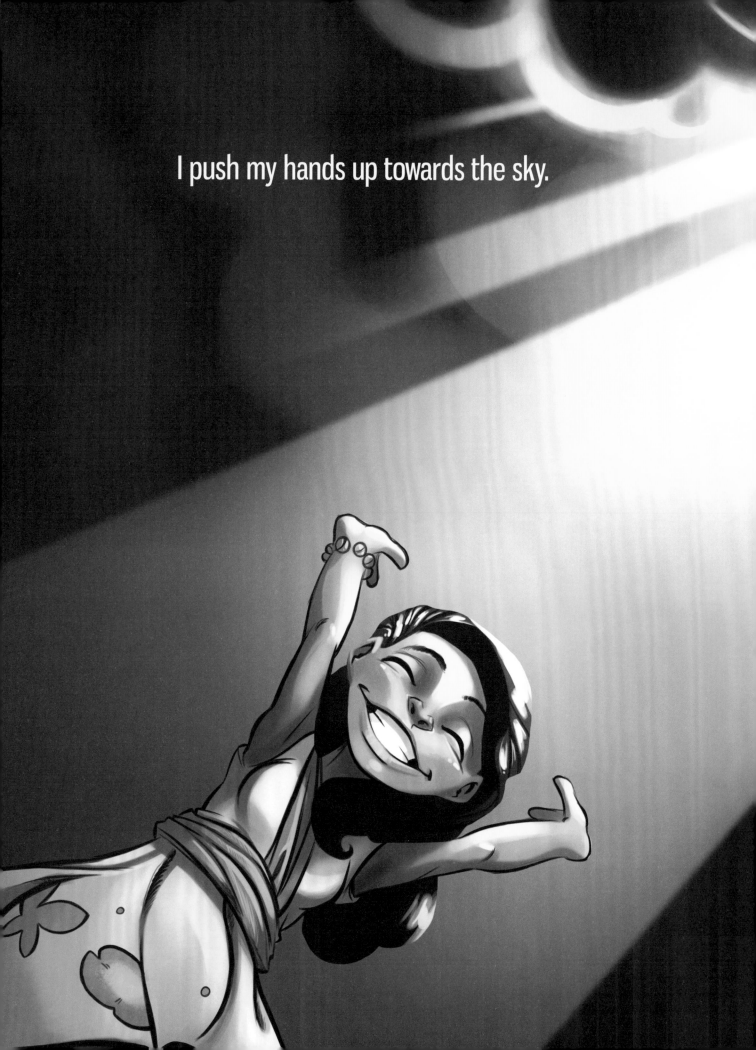

I push my hands up towards the sky.

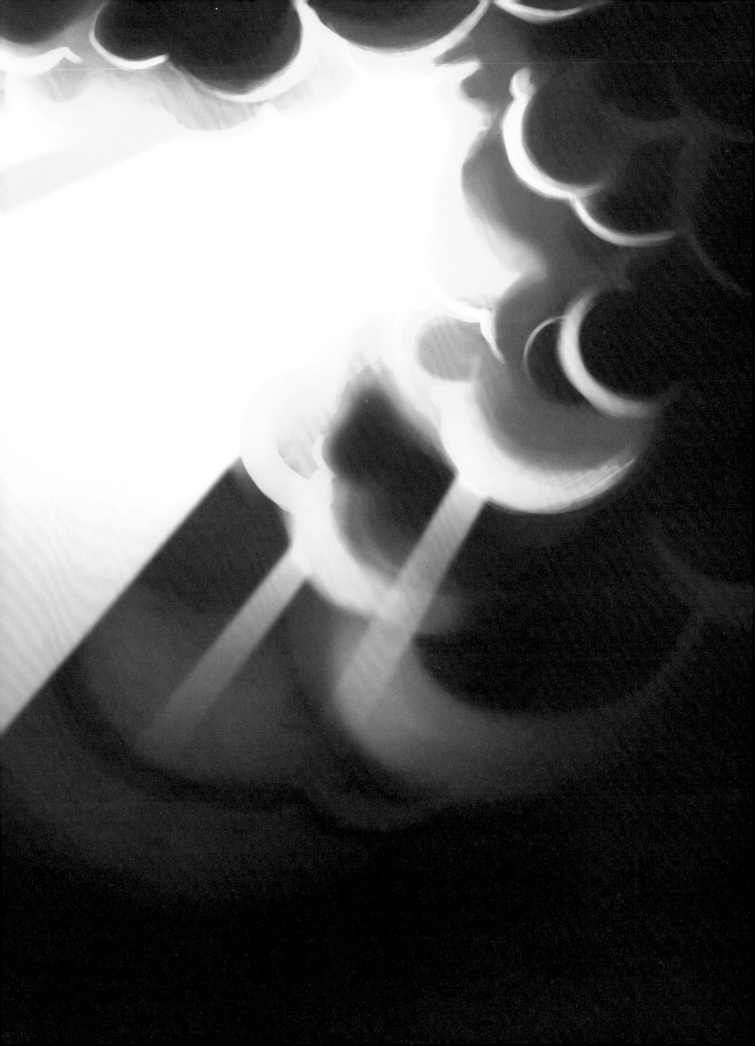

Then slowly I bring them back over my heart.
Breathing in. Breathing out.

I imagine the sun as it starts a new day.
I lift my hands towards the sky,
Stretching them out like the sun rising high.
Breathing in. Breathing out.

I bring my arms to rest on my thighs.
I relax and sway like a leaf in the breeze,

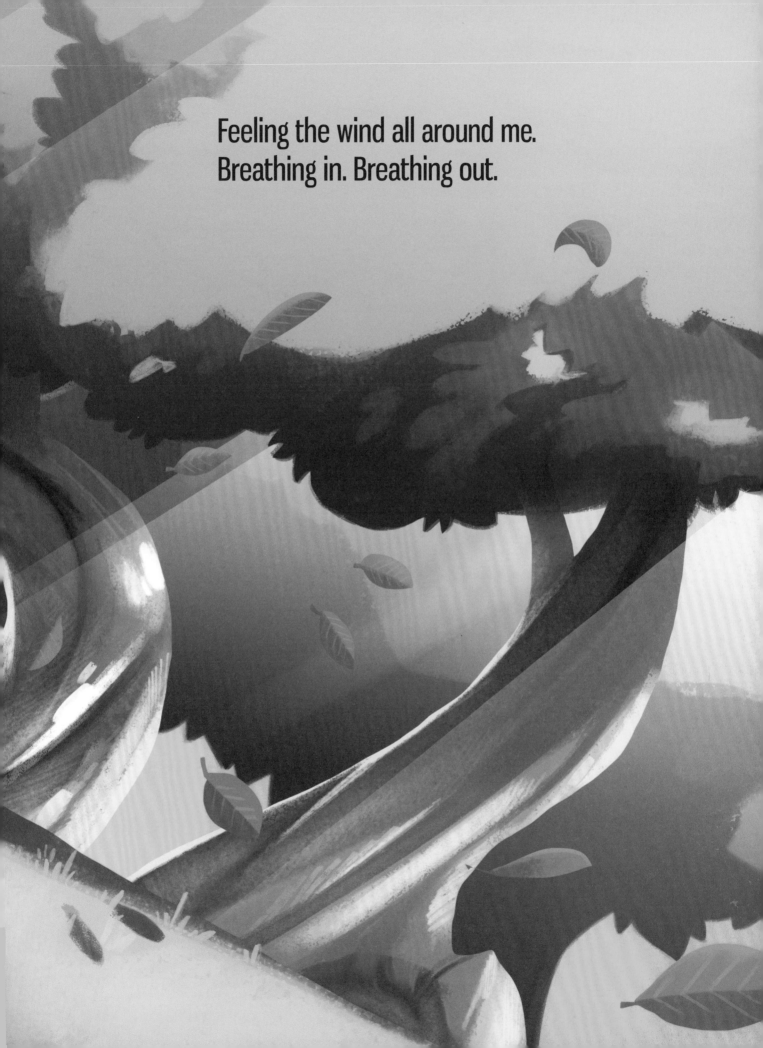

Feeling the wind all around me.
Breathing in. Breathing out.

I reach out slowly as if picking dandelions in the field.
I breathe in and bring the flowers to my mouth.

Then gently blow them out.
Breathing in. Breathing out.

My mind is clear and free like the wind.
I am mindful.

Mindful of who I am,
Mindful of how I control my feelings and thoughts.

Breathing In. Breathing out.
I am lifted.

Up, Up, and Away!
It's time to get back to a great day.

Author's Note

The complexities of emotions can be a daunting challenge for children. Identifying, experiencing, and responding to emotions is further complicated as these precocious and emerging learners try to understand themselves and the world around them. The importance of emotional intelligence and social emotional learning cannot be underestimated, and should be encouraged in the early years and beyond because recognizing their emotions, feelings, and thoughts is an important tool to identify and manage emotions.

Emotional intelligence is recognizing, understanding and managing our emotions, including that of others. Vast research in the field shows that children with higher emotional intelligence, demonstrate an increase in the perceptions of others, show more empathy, build better relationships, have higher grades, and perform better on achievement tests. Overall, raising an emotionally intelligent child prepares them for life's challenges, while building growth-minded, well-rounded children.

Developing children's emotional intelligence is an important factor in overcoming barriers, and adopting healthy behaviors for everyday life. Beyond understanding and balancing their own emotions, they too must see how they interconnect to social interactions (social intelligence), in how we connect with others and their emotions, hence social and emotional intelligence. The linkage of social intelligence–the essential components of emotional communication, can help build or erode relationships.

The themes represented in this book center around mindfulness, emotional intelligence, and social emotional competencies as an opportunity to help children differentiate their emotions, and how they respond to them. As a resource to further support children in identifying their emotions, I have included a set of emotional monsters on the next page. The emotional messages identified and understood helps teach and support self-awareness, self-management, and problem-solving skills to strengthen emotional intelligence and well-being.

Being mindful is being present, a pause in the moment, where in that stillness, we engage our senses to the thoughts, feelings, emotions–the place and space we inhabit at that moment. Through promoting and integrating social and emotional skills utilizing mindfulness, this book helps harness, engage, and strengthen these skills through practice in real and tangible ways.

Social and emotional learning plays a critical role in our homes, communities, schools, and classrooms. Unwind, Up, Up, and Away is a resource for all settings. In education, the Collaborative for Academic, Social, and Emotional Learning (CASEL), "promotes integrated academic, social, and emotional learning for all children in preschool through high school." CASEL identifies five interrelated sets of social and emotional learning competencies: self-awareness, self-management, social awareness, relationship skills, and responsible decision-making. The CASEL SEL wheel and competencies are included in the back of the book.

The integration of social + emotional intelligence in the lives of children helps to set a foundation that contributes to their well-being as they learn and grow, building the skills necessary to help them to thrive in life. Unwind. Up, Up, and Away! is a kid-friendly teachable moment towards lifelong practice and wellness for growing healthy relationships and raising confident kids!

Emotional Monsters

HAPPY   **SAD**   **FEAR**   **NERVOUS**

GRIEF   **OPTIMISTIC**   **PATIENT**   **STRESS**

SHY   **EXCITED**   **CURIOUS**   **SURPRISED**

ANXIOUS   **IRRITATED**   **LONELY**   **COURAGEOUS**

WORRY   **DEFENSIVE**   **BETRAYED**   **PLAYFUL**

CHEERFUL **ASHAMED** **MEAN** **DISAPPOINTED**

FRUSTRATED **DEPRESSED** **WITHDRAWN** **ANGER**

ENVY **ANNOYED** **DISTRACTED** **CALM**

SELFISH **THREATENED** **EMBARRASSED** **TIRED**

BORED **PANICKY** **CONFUSED** **INSPIRED**

Positive choices and emotions – Be mindful...
You have more power than you think!

SOCIAL AND EMOTIONAL LEARNING (SEL) COMPETENCIES

SELF-AWARENESS

The ability to accurately recognize one's own emotions, thoughts, and values and how they influence behavior. The ability to accurately assess one's strengths and limitations, with a well-grounded sense of confidence, optimism, and a "growth mindset."

- ○ IDENTIFYING EMOTIONS
- ○ ACCURATE SELF-PERCEPTION
- ○ RECOGNIZING STRENGTHS
- ○ SELF-CONFIDENCE
- ○ SELF-EFFICACY

SELF-MANAGEMENT

The ability to successfully regulate one's emotions, thoughts, and behaviors in different situations — effectively managing stress, controlling impulses, and motivating oneself. The ability to set and work toward personal and academic goals.

- ○ IMPULSE CONTROL
- ○ STRESS MANAGEMENT
- ○ SELF-DISCIPLINE
- ○ SELF-MOTIVATION
- ○ GOAL SETTING
- ○ ORGANIZATIONAL SKILLS

SOCIAL AWARENESS

The ability to take the perspective of and empathize with others, including those from diverse backgrounds and cultures. The ability to understand social and ethical norms for behavior and to recognize family, school, and community resources and supports.

- ○ PERSPECTIVE-TAKING
- ○ EMPATHY
- ○ APPRECIATING DIVERSITY
- ○ RESPECT FOR OTHERS

RELATIONSHIP SKILLS

The ability to establish and maintain healthy and rewarding relationships with diverse individuals and groups. The ability to communicate clearly, listen well, cooperate with others, resist inappropriate social pressure, negotiate conflict constructively, and seek and offer help when needed.

- ○ COMMUNICATION
- ○ SOCIAL ENGAGEMENT
- ○ RELATIONSHIP BUILDING
- ○ TEAMWORK

RESPONSIBLE DECISION-MAKING

The ability to make constructive choices about personal behavior and social interactions based on ethical standards, safety concerns, and social norms. The realistic evaluation of consequences of various actions, and a consideration of the well-being of oneself and others.

- ○ IDENTIFYING PROBLEMS
- ○ ANALYZING SITUATIONS
- ○ SOLVING PROBLEMS
- ○ EVALUATING
- ○ REFLECTING
- ○ ETHICAL RESPONSIBILITY

© CASEL 2017

A portion of proceeds
from this book will support the

CHRISTOPHER
GATES
FOUNDATION

Inspiring generosity, encouraging activism,
and empowering sustainability through
collaborative partnerships and outreach initiatives
that impact the world, by effective and proactive giving.